THE LITMUS BODY

Other Poetry Titles from Quarry Press

THE LITMUS BODY

NADINE McINNIS

For Vickey:

An earlier (and darker)
vision.

All the best,

Nadine

March 9, 1998

QUARRY PRESS

Some of these poems have appeared in *Arc, Canadian Woman Studies, Dandelion, Event, The Fiddlehead, Grain, Contemporary Verse II, Poetry Canada Review, Prairie Fire, Quarry, Room of One's Own,* and *The University of Windsor Review,* and in the anthologies *Capital Poets: An Ottawa Anthology* (Ouroboros, 1989), *More Garden Varieties* (Aya,The League of Canadian Poets, 1989), and *Garden Varieties 4* (Sono Nis, The League of Canadian Poets, 1992). The poem "reliquary" was a first prize winner in the Ottawa and Region C.A.A. poetry competition.

The author would like to thank the Ontario Arts Council for a Works-in-Progress grant and the Regional Municipality of Ottawa-Carleton for a Senior Artists' Grant as well as to the vital writing community of Ottawa for stimulation and support, particularly to John Barton, Colin Morton, Sandra Nicholls, and Blaine Marchand for their friendship and advice, and to Melanie Dugan of Quarry Press for her editorial assistance. A special thanks to Jennifer Dickson.

The publisher acknowledges the financial assistance of The Canada Council and the Ontario Arts Council.

Canadian Cataloguing in Publication Data
    McInnis, Nadine, 1957 —
      The litmus body

    Poems.
    ISBN 1-55082-037-0

     I. Title.

    PS8575.I54L48 1992 C811'.54 C92-090057-7
    PR9199.3.M34L48 1992

Cover art entitled "Death by Water: Three (Masks)," from the original hand-tinted etching by Jennifer Dickson, 1979, reproduced by permission of the artist and The Canada Council Art Bank.

Design by Keith Abraham. Typeset by Susan Hannah.
Printed and bound in Canada by Hignell Printing,
Winnipeg, Manitoba.

Published by Quarry Press, Inc., P.O. Box 1061,
Kingston, Ontario K7L 4Y5.

*For Tim Fairbairn,
and our children,
Nadia and Owen*

Contents

III A Woman Writes About Fire

IV Generation

I
Birthmark

birthmark

you say it is the shape of Antarctica
my birthmark
stretched over one hip
some outpost sends signals
your tongue   surfaces
nimble as a seal

but I hear too
the silences between us
dry valleys where no rain has fallen
in two million years
each of us wanders alone
longing to hear another human voice

where is the magnetic pole we search for?
our children stretching up between us
drift and lean toward
maturity   those far-off solar storms
unfelt by us

long after they are gone
I'll still be marked with streaks
ridges of mountains   uninhabited now
and an older mark too
the birthmark of all women
that stains the imaginations of men

am I still so unknown?
expanse of chilly fissures
raucous calls of my voice wheeling around you
spine turned away in the long dark

just as easily
it could be seen otherwise
soothing shadow of the baobab tree
at high noon
the outline of a turtle
dragging herself back to the warm sea
relieved of her worry of eggs

let us inhabit any land
but this one   of whiteouts
islands of deception
you must chisel and blast and drag
yourself with ropes away from
a wind change   caprice of nature
binds you to me again

exiled here with weather watchers
a few twisted life forms
hunched between rocks
I see you across distances
reclining with the lions under that baobab tree
although our bodies nudge in sleep
the slow drift of continents
together and apart

incantations: crossing over

1

in the season of dying fireflies
your father's seeds forming by the second
    a thousand times one   a thousand times two
    a thousand times three
far off   like thunder.
I know the smell   buckwheat honey
last pollen fermenting in dark hives
and something cold too   ice fog rolling in
or snow storming into the black river
before the freeze

we pass before your sister
groggy with heat and television
we pass   clouds effacing the light on her face
then gone
    a thousand and one   a thousand
    and two
sheets pushed below our feet peak into whitecaps
his mouth on my breasts   a few damp gusts
promising
still far off
thunder

threadlike roots prickle my skin
I loosen and rise like damp soil   as a root
eases deeper   I make way
Lightning.   does it gather underground
finding its effortless way to the charged sky
only appearing to strike from airy heights?
whatever way   the great tree splits
earth and sky open together with light
    a thousand and one   it travels across our faces
    a thousand   thousand   thousand

2

here is the dark current
    you must struggle against
and here is a planet
    warmed by the sun
then lurching towards night,
cities
    like phosphorescent barnacles
    hooked onto its scarred sides

    come closer
though you will not see us
arms around each other
    under the dim willows

only the high bright voice
of your sister   singing
    along shore   as she stirs
the inky current with a stick

    come closer
you must see through our eyes
    and choose   streetlights
curved stamens over the bridge
scattering light onto the river

see the other shore
    spotlights aimed at a church
hiss in metal cages
    before settling quietly
at dawn

we all contain
our tense quota of unused light
    channelled by our minds
    into these simple circuits

so much remains   straining
        to spill out of our bodies
our hearts   *come closer*
to the flawless bridges
        on fire inside every bulb

too bright to face
        without shade   *cross over*
as we each did alone
                cross over

3

by the ochre spotlights
of the museum
    you see the curio bones
    no-one mourns
and start to turn away

hot wax   seeps
dark
    from your guttering flame
moving towards extinction
and not even bones will remain

a sudden chill of shaking
    exiting
under the red lettered light
    mounted above the tunnel
leading to the room of artifacts
hot black wax
    runs out of my body

Halloween tomorrow
    the night the dead
are most active   knock
and knock and knock
    and who is there?   no-one
no-one at all

    turn back
each of us knows who carves
the grimace of the jack-o-lantern
    we see fibrous chambers
smashed all over roads
    the morning after

    turn back   to the surgeon
who cut the mouth in my ripeness

    turn back   to your sister
who blazed out of me
    a howl of light

turn back   to your father
warming my hands

turn back   to me   lying here
in the room of emergencies

I see the light   too
        overhead   a cool tube
        nailed tongue to tail
trembling
        as though it is afraid

4

over the body   hot and fragile
    as blown glass
he moves the sound crystal
as though clearing an iced window

    someone is there
in the dark womb   continent
usually uninhabited
where no living thing can winter
    but a tiny shape
    transparent as an ice fish
flickering beneath the blizzards
    that bind the frigid seas

    someone is there   turning back
toward this square of light
my body   pane of flesh
    I see you through
leaning against the stinging
    sweep of stars
flushed out into blackness
    rope at your waist
reeling yourself back
to the tree by the door

how it groans
    toward the cold earth
    someone is there   you can see them
moving in and out of view
your father   sister
    settling into evening
behind a window   and your mother's face
close to the pane
    searching the dark for a shape
struggling into human form

you   too   can watch me form
      in the physical world
a face   still obscured
by the pallor of the spirit
      who will glide to your bedside
years from now   a cool hand
soothing your brow

5

The solstice arrives;
all over our house bulbs burn out.
One by one, your sister unscrews them,
showing me dusty black bruises inside glass,
shakes them close to her ear
and laughs at the far-off tinkling of reindeer,
to me, the sound of the Salvation Army
on street corners, their glass globes
filling slowly with loose change,
bells summoning random, transitory love.
Some shivering soul will have a roof overhead
tonight.

There is a tree in our livingroom
strung with coloured bulbs that by turn
grow dull and cold, but you, gathering strength,
have your own tree sparkling with nutrients and cells.
Behind you, double helix, tricky bridge you crossed upon,
and ahead, the gruelling ascent from my body
into the acid light, and much further ahead
there will be old age,
the river below us passing beneath ice,
my ribs, the bones of my hands
standing out like intricate girders of a bridge
still incomplete,   ending   mid-air

6

voluptuous
the swirl forming again

a funnel lengthening
stretches down
joining sky and earth

I curl over you   unborn
shelter your body with mine
endure the force
before it lifts and passes on
the world reorganises
nurses offer crushed ice
your father fiddles
with the dial of a radio

clouds swirl again
this time   sickening
black funnel eases down
I curve over your body
can barely hear over the roar
a weather report   *the great lakes*
dairy country   georgian bay
owen sound   your name
the funnel ripping open graves
on hillsides
my grandfather rises
his name torn from him
by this wind
flung at you
still unborn
owen   the sky clears

one breath   two breaths
I look up
damp gusts swirling again
a funnel pulling air into it
I gasp   it touches and lifts
touches and lifts   touches
and lifts
owen sound over the air waves
storm warning   a squall
your cry thudding onto shore
and me   still arced
denying over and over
that sound
is your voice
where are you?   far away
in *owen sound*   your round face
the wavering reflection of the moon

A dairy farm near the lake has passed
down through generations.

A stranger lies curled against a woman,
light breeze off the water lifting curtains,
carrying to him the pungence of newly turned loam.

He does not know he smells it.   He is asleep.

All night, I hear traffic moving by on Main Street,
light from the hall illuminating curtains
around my bed as they breathe slowly,
in and out, recirculated hospital air.
A radio at the nurses' station turned low,
hour by hour, a forecast passes through my mind:
pressures, gradual clearing, eventually frost
in outlying areas but wherever you lie,
calm and bright tonight.

A radio turns itself on: *the great lakes*
dairy country   georgian bay   owen sound
He listens and stirs, cattle swollen full and restless.

He steps into the barn at the moment
they place you in my arms for the first time,
your small quavering voice breaking with the dawn.
He thinks he hears a baby far off,
maybe above in the hay mow, but lowers his head,
spills more milk into a pail,   the wavering cry
of a rooster summoning the light of another
ordinary day.

a wolf trails every woman

a wolf trails every woman
after she gives birth
he picks up her scent the first time
she pulls herself to her feet

and her bright blood
rushes through newly opened channels
this is the sad hemophilia
she will drag behind her from now on

occasionally   during labour
she hears the child's heart
tracked on its last mysterious wanderings
inside her   and suddenly the wolf

appears   the child's heart thumps
a startled deer
dashing out of range
and all she can do is listen

she delivers howls of rage
snarls challenge the wolf's dominance
for a moment she's stronger
than any other on earth

but the wolf paces himself
she is vulnerable now that she's
opened up
he could find her anywhere

protected by a circle of women
for her body emits
a high-pitched scream
only he can hear

the sweet scented baby is rocked
passed from arms to arms
she poises ready to snatch him back
and flee

in the heart of a city
she listens in her sleep
jumps at the revving of cars
the aimless barking of chained dogs

the opening of flowers

a gentle easing
invisible as the hour hand
passing
but for the new mother
holding her sleeping baby
the last of the hospital bouquet
to open in her livingroom
tremble
green tipped pods   tight
and the stretching
petals starting to differentiate
turn slowly outwards
soft and pale as the skin
of her inner thighs
and she slows her breathing
to let it come
rises and leaves the room
but the flowers are inside her
their perfume
sharp as alcohol
and her house is filled
with their groans

cry

These toys
have already given you a taste for power,
but it is their emptiness
forcing itself out in cries for mercy;
asthmatic wheeze of the dinosaur,
the panda squashed beneath you,
slow exhalation, an agony of protest.
All the creatures of this earth
scaled down to fit your clumsy grip.
The air you squeeze out through tiny holes
smells stale as the air that circles
endlessly in a parking garage
where someone has been loitering
waiting for a woman to happen by
alone

but the toys cry because they are empty.

I must teach you to be gentle, and not
to tear at my lower lip with your nails
when I try to rock you to sleep in my arms,
not to twist the free nipple when you suck,
as though there is something denied you,
something more desired locked inside.
There is no lost part of you in me.
You took everything with you when you left,
dragging that great weight of independence
on a rope behind you. I must teach you that
a woman's cry does not rise from an empty space
you can leave behind.   A woman
is not just empty space you can tear open
and fill.

watching her swim

My daughter has learned to swim today
in a vaporous lake heavy as mercury,
her baby cheeks puffing, ineffectual
wind demon, stirring up a trail of froth
that dissolves and forgets her.

I sit on a rock, smile turned outward,
with fingernails cutting my palms, learning,
as she is, the skill of letting go;
to move without alarm, breathe slow as a reptile
sunning on the edge of this precambrian bowl.

Today, even the inorganic is in flux.
Clouds ionize darkness, ink out light
with a high black heat. Broken boulders
thirty feet under are closed fists that do not care
to hold her up as a mother would.

Silver flickers by, storms hardening
year after year to the agelessness of ice. Many
have drifted down, bodies nudging rock, knocking
to be let in but without force. The dead
are almost weightless at such a depth.

She struggles against the cold slap on the skin
of wave after wave. That smooth brow,
faintly blue, recedes between exertions.
Easily, she could slip beneath the surface
alchemy of storm and light, and leave me here,

alone, diving into the iron-laden water,
cold passing through my hands, numbing my arms,
eyes darkening orange, then red, blacking out
in a faint as I did after her birth, groping,
blind, through the old blood she came from.

ice storm: christmas eve

she believes this season;
the letter laboured with red crayon
is sent off like a prayer

thin wafers of shortbread, milk,
apple for the reindeer
left near the window

she waits out a flushed happy sleep
as ice sizzles in the trees,
blue sparks leap twig to twig

after midnight, trunks and branches
split under the sheer weight
of all that shimmering beauty

by morning, the apple is gone,
a glass, clouded with breath
rolls under a chair

she wakes to a cold house,
candles by nightfall,
but all her presents intact

puzzles, their little bones rattling,
a baby doll, cool as wax
and the trees along her street

exploded in glittering clouds,
limbs hurled at caved-in roofs,
black power lines looped on lawns

dangerous graffiti,
a hissing line coils
around the neighbour's snowman

this is how her letter is answered.

what angry herds trampled
the arboretum of her city last night,
left antlers splintered on river banks

she plays with new picture blocks,
ordering disturbed nature:
little feet of the newborn lamb,

the shepherd's staff
and here
is where the spring sun goes

but who in such a hurry
crushed cars with heavy feet,
was that wind

the howling of reindeer,
those loud sounds she dreamt,
whip cracks on their bloody backs?

reliquary

Crosses are vanishing
from above doorways and beds.
Instead, each of us lives
with a humming vault in our kitchens
the size of our own coffin,
its perpetual drone
like the ringing in the ears
of explorers before they freeze
or go mad.

This is a tall icy country
either in total darkness
or total light
with no line possible between.
Children put eyes to the slit,
pull slowly
to catch light snapping on.
Never are they thin or fast
enough

and the few who crawl inside
hurtle into their past
are found curled, blue chicks
feathered with frost, in eggs
that will never hatch,
and only melons
withering in the crisper
remember how they got there.

We were warned about this
even before kidnappers,
yet our crayon suns and flower bursts
were drawn to its magnetic pole.
Like mothers before me
I tape her feverish colours onto white,
a shrine to her quick vision,
a prayer that cold also preserves.

fable

what shape did you imagine
coming for you out of the snow
as I prepared to leave
your tiny face
pressed against glass

what's wrong?   and you said
almost under your breath:
the baby slitter is coming

how could I not laugh
robbing language of its terror
its power

and how could I not laugh
when you searched
for your library book on its
day doomed
because it had to go back
to where it came from

write a story so that children
won't get hurt
or taken away
you tell me as you leave for school

so I begin
to write a fable at that moment
I know you are standing on the road

the entrance to the park
is to your left

you give it wide berth
wait for the traffic to clear
and turn towards school

remember this fable
on the day I am unable
to imagine where you might be

on the day you turn left
instead of right

following the twisted path
that leads to the river:

A little girl is lost in a city park. The trees lift their bare limbs in a
sour wind that blows around the planet, picking up the scent of
deserts and factories and the moldy smell of old mine shafts. Every
time she closes her eyes, she thinks she might be somewhere dif-
ferent; the dust bowl of Africa, she thinks, or the raw green edge
of stripped rain forest, but when she opens her eyes, there is only
the snowy park, and she is alone. Men in uniform are dragging
the black river for the body of a woman last seen balanced on the
railing of a bridge. She hopes it is not her mother. She doesn't go
near. The moon above is milky white, suddenly blocked by a man
hanging over her like a shabby shadow. She backs away, feels the
chainlink fence biting into her shoulders and wonders if he will
leave her alone if she is polite, if she says *please*. As his hands
come out of his pockets, a voice calls across the snow: *Hey!*, and
he turns, spits words that she's seen scrawled under the bridge,
then shrinks away when he sees the whirling shape, an animal
blur of fur circling, tracking by scent. The girl lifts her eyes, and
there she is; a fierce young woman with white hair spiked around
her head like solar eclipse. From her ear hangs a starfish on a
chain. *Your mother sent me,* she says. Then she whistles, and the
animal leaps into her arms, nuzzles back inside her coat as she
stoops to help the child stand. *It's a ferret. Do you want to hold it?*
The young woman unbuttons her coat and the child is surprised
by how soft and white her breasts are. The ferret's claws have left
red dents, but the skin isn't broken. The child forgets she is lost.
She touches its slinky, quivering length, so furtive and explosive
under her small hand. *If you're not afraid, it can help you,* and she
places the ferret inside the child's coat, warm, where her breast
will grow one day. The woman walks away and leaves her, the
ferret curled next to her heart.

II
Purification

purification

The technician
peering into the canister
of calm water
doesn't measure how toxins
pass like thoughts
through her tiny wrinkled brain.
All he sees is a litmus body
with no soul
in the shape
of a small fish.

The plant will open valves
to the river
if she survives the night.
He doesn't know
that she feels spring break-up
as a far-off shudder
in her gills,
making her dizzy,
but notes that her belly
is pulled upwards
by the antigravity
of death
as she struggles
to swim straight.

She is clarifying her blood
of his PCBs, his DDTs.
She is ridding herself
of his language.
One hour more
and he'll open valves,
flush her out,
an inch of flesh
in a torrent of rusty metal,
rubber, ice chunks
grey with exhaust.

He could never know
that she's dreamed
of this
all her still life,
that she's dreamed too
of the hook dangling
like a question mark
he tosses so casually
from overpasses,
tearing her heart from her
with one sharp tug.

blasting river ice

I

In the no man's land of midafternoon
the shore is crowded.
Women with children in tow
watch the workers far out on the ice
with their giant buzzsaw cutting keys.
Black water seeps through slits
as the river creaks and stirs.

The workers move like women
gently lifting children from a van,
The Powder Co. Limited, a motto on its doors,
they drag red sleds to the edge.

Easily, she could let herself follow,
dragging the weight of her daughter,
rope cutting just under her heart.
She could send her into the black current
with one smooth shove.

A shudder up her spine, snow drifts
down the back of her neck like the powder
she's smoothed onto her daughter's skin
since birth. Heart lit with tenderness
but some thing else too, burning
like a fuse along her arteries.
All along the shore she hears women
ticking   ticking

The blast travels along the river bottom,
breaks the trance of fish,
gills suddenly strain against sleep
and they awaken to cold, darkness
a jagged sphere of light,
its chunky corona of ice
swirls overhead.

2

A cloud of scorched ice crystals
hangs over the park.
The air darkens with fantasies.

Each blast opens a brittle cell
in her mind.
Images flash
in perfect clarity.

Tomorrow is the day
she must sort through her daughter's
fairytales and summer clothes,
taking only essentials.

First thing in the morning
she will clear her kitchen shelves
of the sherries, cut crystal
that ease her through that hour of dusk.

A few strong swings of his golfclub
and the leap of spirits would shatter
before crashing, formless,
the smell of fruits and flowers,
ruby and rising in heat waves
from shards of glass,

ice
pushed
onto her bleeding feet.

3

The daughter waits.

She is three
and has learned secrecy.

When her mother is beyond caring,
muttering, her forehead resting
against the living room window,
she opens the passageway to the river,
surface faintly rippled
as though shaken by flickers of tails
hidden around the blue porcelain curve.

She wants them to rise to her,
to the light and heat and food
the river   locked in ice   cannot offer.

She sprinkles goldfish food
and waits.

Half the box gone now,
swirling in small circles
clots, useless.

She flushes,
her chin on the rim.
A face,
fractured scales of light,
swarms and reforms,
stares back from still water.

4

When first she brought them home
to her daughter
they snapped back
from the sides of the bowl.
One day of fury, while the others,
tarnished and wild, slept
near river bottoms.

Some nights she dreams
the bowl crumbles in her hands,
fish, marbles, bloodwarm water
spill onto her feet.
She dreams
they are pierced with sewing needles.

Her daughter watches them
more closely than she dares,
says: *They're calling you.*
Look at their mouths,
they're saying MOM   MOM   MOM

5

She paces
with a thrashing under her breast
as the blasting shakes her windows,

turns the six o'clock news up loud,
speaker aimed at the fish
but nothing agitates them now.
They stopped growing
weeks ago.

When will it be over.   How long
can it take to open a channel
that runs black and strong
for only one short season.

What is the point, she wonders,
of freeing a river
that in the heart of summer
quickly clogs with duckweed.

After that, the quick cooling,
icy shards spreading towards the middle
like brittle shadows of all the women
who have passed afternoons on shore
waiting.

6

They move the fishbowl
to the bathroom where the net is left
within reach.

Her daughter knows now
that the river cannot flow to her
but has dreamed of the fish
landing in a cloud of bubbles
in the whirlpool under the bridge,
two gold lights spinning away.

When her bed rocks gently
and her small limbs are released
to the cool currents of sheets,
she sees her fish flicker by,
grown long and sleek to fit the river.

In the morning she scurries to the bathroom
before waking her mother
but no matter how fast she moves
they are always there
before her,
suspended in their trance,
coming around sleepily to glide up
and kiss the ends of her fingers,
as though they haven't moved
the whole night long.

swans

The swans snort through wax museum beaks
with an aged weariness.

Their scaled feet,
the tired feet of dinosaurs

dragging a heaviness out of the river
for our scraps, our sugary wastes.

Swans, coiled under the willows, wait
with eyes tucked under flightless wings.

Sun slants beneath the bridge
sending its heat back to the stars.

The swans do not care. Their eggs are
soft hidden skulls cooling in the rushes.

Soon the trucks will come, leaving scars
in the river's sides, and the men

with their needles of dreamless sleep
will lower them,

gently,
onto the concrete of winter pens.

sheep

she's shut away pills
       the last dry pebbles at
the bottom of a glass

well   she's closed
       the top on the cloud
of cotton   caught as

it drifts over   the
       fleece of sheep frozen
mid-leap   the sheep

that her mother told
       her to count   not back
wards for the rush of

anaesthetic   but for
       wards   herds of them
in holding pens   all

the sleepless nights
       all the pills flank to
flank follow her every

where a racket in her
       purse   sharp hooves
rattle on rock   her

heart shakes like the
       ground under a stampede
she can hear mournful

calling near the rail
       way   yards   slats narrow
her vision   chutes

deliver them   one by one to
        senselessness   she's pushed
to that chute by a crush

of bodies   the mirror
        slices her pale face
at four in the morning

she reaches

the mirror in her bathroom
        creaks open   a freezer lid
resisting   resisting

feast

"Then came in all the king's wise men,
but they could not read the writing:
nor make known to the king
the interpretation of it."
                    Daniel, 5:8

(and who can read the writing on the wall   while the rest
of us feast and praise our gods of gold and iron?)

can the woman full with child
in the richest country in the world
who doesn't eat a thing
with pleasure
but ice
chipped in secret from her fridge
with a butter knife
or ashes
from the fireplace
she kneels on the plush broadloom with a spoon
and tastes
her lips blackening with delight

can the child
in the richest country in the world
who eats earth
under the perfumed shadows of the rose garden
mimicking the child
on the other side of the planet
who digs for ungerminated seeds in the dust

welcome to the feast:

at high noon   on a platform before a cheering crowd
you can have
17 plates of spaghetti   eaten with your hands
tied behind your back
you can break records
you can eat a 1958 Chevy truck over the course of 3 weeks
and be famous for it

or

you can lie down in the shade of a rock
too weak to catch the flies that swarm along your eyelids
you'd eat them   but now   you're too slow

for siesta   you can have a woman
bury your face in her genitals
like she's a thing you've hunted down

or

you can have what the drain catches
from the noontime dishes
soapy shreds of lettuce and ham   a swollen tea bag
if only someone would ship it to you

later   you can have
12 little birds all on one plate
24 little wings set aside
without the faintest blemish of teeth marks

or you can have *take out*   burgers
or Chinese driven to your door
without a charge
take out rain forests   take out villages
put in dust dust ashes and dust

(who can read these flyers
that fall into your home
unbidden?   too many   too much bother)

perhaps only the wolf you've chased from your door can
who slips down from the hills at midnight
to feast on afterbirth
shovelled out of the barn
the wolf who knows all about hunger and hunting
the wolf who knows his brothers   his enemies
and knows nothing should be wasted
who slips down from the hills at midnight
to eat the richest food on earth
knowing food is found gold
knowing food is pure power

conscience

The sea has swallowed its fill.
It curdles, and coughs up on beaches
vials of infected blood, sodden gauze,
the lining of a human stomach.
Fetuses, in their element of death,
escape from the limbo their mothers
still need to believe in.
It sickens him how they reach shore
in the excrement of baby sharks.
Although he doesn't know it yet,
as he stands at his office window,
his stomach is turning.

The sun drops pale as a tablet
into the fizzing and foaming sea.
His stomach is pitted with acid,
hunches in his body like the shell
of the hospital he walks towards,
grey and eroded in rain crawling
down his face, perforating stone,
creeping up to rot the atmosphere.

The sterile light of the hospital
purifies his pain. He rises
from his bed, feeling much better
now that the sea has taken on
his burden.
Flowers around his bed crumble;
birds of paradise collapse on slippery
stalks, roses brown like bad teeth
before petals loosen, drop to the floor.

All his possessions in cellophane,
carefully, he zips the bag shut,
back turned to the window
and the grey smudge above the buildings
that is all he knows of the Atlantic.

But his stomach is turning,
turning back towards land, riding in
on the surf in a swell of sea-sickness.
Suddenly, a wave of vertigo.
He lowers his sweating brow and waits
for it to pass, but his stomach
is turning, faster than the earth.

he steps into place

She recognizes him immediately.
He steps into place, positioning his black shoes
in smooth indentations on the other side of the mirror,

but it's not enough.

She wants the reflection unblemished.
She wants to sweep away the forcefield
        of dust
pulsing like membrane between their two worlds.

His hand rises to meet her hand. Two rags
shadow-dancing on the surface of the mirror,
        never touching.
A slim millimetre between them
blurred with imperfection.

Trailing her hand are murky streaks,
currents of debris picked up by a twister,
the whole disarrayed world
he's brought into focus.

And she begins to resent the high polish
        of his shoes
standing solid on cooled volcanic rock.

He follows her every move, willing her
to clear the film from her own eyes.
So she narrows the gap, she reaches for him,
and the glass, rubbed down to absolute clarity
cries out under their hands.

handprint

I saw a man's handprint
burned into the bleached frost of a door
on the coldest night of the year
fingers spread   and every line on his palm
a seam where night seeped through

he was a man of his generation
mount of the moon   blank
untroubled by visions
middle joint of science   prominent
then I saw the deep line of fate:
death by misadventure

who to warn

a man
walking outside the engineering building
on the coldest night of the year

all over the city   car batteries are dead
he and hundreds more set out on foot
furious with what they own
full of acid
their touch burning frosted glass
bodies of women   corroding
night by night

I put my small hand to his cold print
measuring
as though no glass stretches between us
but he could be anywhere by now
this angry man   holding a charge
so strong
he cannot contain it

purgatory for indifferent fathers

some of you will winter on Antarctica
        with an egg balanced on your webbed feet
            and black swords of bitter wind
        will carve most of your body away

        by spring   you'll be a sack of oily feathers
        too weary to protest
            when the mothers return
        sweep hatchlings under their wings
            to live with them at sea

some of you will flay your bodies against cliffs
        on your journey upriver
            even the gentle current in rest pools
        will throb at your slashed sides

some of you will witness this journey
        your faces   chiselled in rock
            looking out through waterfalls
        the tears you had no time for   will pour
            down your faces
        smoothing you down at last

some of you will give your seed reluctantly
            the spasm diminishing you
        held within the many legs of the female
            who revolves above you   huge
            as the sun and the moon

some of you will be spurned by her
        for faults you cannot fathom
            tail feathers not straight enough
            your fur   not pale enough
            your voice   a screechy complaint
        she turns away from with indifference

some of you will be eaten by her

some of you will be invisible to her
       and trillions of tiny statues made in your image
          crouched in the heads of your sperm
       will crumble
          and be reabsorbed into the universe

retracing steps

1

during the ghostly female nights
of the hospital
brides   mothers and frail girls
kidnapped in nightclothes
wander confused in the corridors

the sleeves of the nurses
are soft cobwebs adjusting blankets
their breath on my cheek
a sweet milky cloud in the darkness
whispering   *forget everything*

and on the surface of the water
in a paper cup is a blankness
where my face begins   slowly
to form

white tablets release a dreamless
pallor to faces faintly blue
as the underlip of a snowdrift

women   white echoes

and those of us
who will not let go
curl in our rumpled pale firmaments
still floating in salty silence

are only halfway there

2

you are only here during daylight
with curtains drawn
elected to this dim office
where days come and go
different people come and go
with their worries   laments

>   *more light is needed*
>   *children are at risk*
>
>   *everything is going*
>   *downhill*

so quiet   you draw from me
far more than words
my wrists   inner arms turning to you
like sickly vines
my pale throat longing to let go
its torrent   its pulse
backed up in wan green veins

but you only mirror me
placing yourself opposite my own
mirror
tunnel of frames curving out of sight

at first   I see you clearly
defined and efficient
in your dark suit
but behind you   a flash of a figure
stooped over gleaming machinery
that darkens to tarnished silver
the scalpels   hooks
laid out like heirlooms
fade as the framed men blur
and distance themselves

I am moving away from you
faster than the speed of light
and time turns backwards

around a gloomy bend
something glows red
a leech   bleeding the past
a torch   a wailing
shivers the glass   stained
green as crushed herbs

3

led to sit with you
by ether in its canisters of outer space
by opiates   by sweat and humours
by chanting and trembling
by fire   by drowning
by women slit in soundproof chambers
by the busy corridors below
where hearts stop hourly
and are flogged like slaves
to row some more   by this talking
nothing but talk
by the thin slivers of light
your wrists   like moons
waning in your dark sleeves
and I long to place my lips on that chill
leave the clamour of earth below

but a crane drags its shadow
across drawn curtains
and the jackhammers start again above us

there is never enough room
others are waiting
you say   and smile

I turn away to leave
ice crystals fogging the glass
around my head
my heart   a bowl of dust

4

for your office you have learned
the discipline of four languages

      It is not enough.

the hieroglyphics of chemistry

      It is not enough.

the yoga of steady hands

      It is not enough.

the drama of masks

      It is not enough.

your torch burns down and flickers
like a firefly at the crossroads
as I tunnel my way
through this dark valley
and the frames shatter
a city collapsing   shaken
by some wave passing through bedrock

we stumble free of the ruined hospital
and become two passersby
hearing a baby's cry beneath the rubble

a cry
wilder than any siren
uttering the oath of all living things

we grub with our torn hands
down towards the cry
and drag it feet first
into our damaged world

III

A Woman Writes About Fire

a woman writes about fire

Old houses have their hidden sources

she checks the steady blue flame
inside the oven
before sliding in her bread

pilot light   calm
unwavering millimetre   god
invisible to all but those
who squat and search

then she sits at the table to write
recalling the voices of the fire
cackling snapping laughter
shaking the grain elevator

genesis: a few scattered grains
quivering sparks igniting dim air

and writes:

> fire never finds
> enough places to live
>
> cannot stand the idleness
> of empty buildings
>
> fire wants to put things to use
> to tell us stories

she's heard people in the Chinese cafe
say a black figure slipped into the graveyard
five minutes after the elevator went up

she's seen people shrug and say:

> *Isn't it strange*
> *how all the pigeons flew away*
> *the day before*
>
> *as if they knew*

flew cross-country to the empty barn
beside her house
their muscular rotations   grey vapours
in upper air ribbed with light

lately   they've been disappearing
as if they sense the barn
smoulders
towards its moment

she wants to stop fiery squatters
from claiming her barn
and puts it to use   though fire doesn't care
how she loves the round knocking
of her boots on tamarack logs,
how the rust from old tools
sticks to her fingers like pollen,
gets all over her papers

the pigeons have moved into her attic
coo to each other
as though the house is empty
as it was for years

twice   fire has leapt onto cellar walls
she's turned her stinging face
to its sagging belly of red pipes

could not discover from the fire's dying voice
whether the story
was to be about the house
or about herself:
the stranger burned in her bed before dawn
and not a soul within three miles

can already hear the faint whine
of voices in the cafe
wheeling around her like flies:

>   *Odd, a woman, all alone*

>   *Heard she set it herself*

>   *No.   Made it out to the roof*
>   *before her nightgown caught fire*

she takes her bread out of the oven
sits again   and writes:

>   fire
>   go hiss elsewhere

>   I live here now
>   I tell my own stories

>   fire give me time

model home 1

When we came here, only the sewers were complete.
A water-purification plant near the river
seen from my bedroom window;
gas flame, tethered by one foot to a water-tower,
wings flapping on fire,
and darkness all along the crescent.

Eerie, when the model homes were locked
and left for the night. No neighbours yet,
just model homes, with ropes cordoning
tastefully furnished rooms. How could we resist
leaving our mark on lush carpets,
the kitchens, so well-equipped,
but only sawdust inside cupboards.

We were like the only survivors of a bomb
that leaves buildings intact.
What allowed us to remain so untouched
by the waves that sweep the living away?

model home 2

From this window, I watch the bones
of half-erected houses flesh out
with siding and shingles and secrecy.
The model homes are occupied now;
delicate shapes glide behind glass, backs turned
on the rest of us as the fruit trees
are swaddled against coming cold.

I lie in bed
watching an aquarium hidden in my closet
glow green beside my new shoes.
The last angel fish, all skull and withered
shank, almost unable to turn now in shrunken water.
Bones of the dead melt mercifully away,

while they circle downstairs;   my father
leaving a trail of water rings,
my mother following just out of sight, wiping,
scouring, dragging the vacuum like a branch
over the snowy carpet, erasing every trace
that we ever passed this way.

model home 3

On Saturdays,
my mother watches our neighbour mow his lawn,
the tiny scars all over his torso standing out
white as his back browns.

Her skin is always flawless, an even tan.
When she lies under the bars in the salon,
maybe she imagines his body
with the scars that look like jaggedly healed
rips of shark's teeth.
He gives her something to think about;
shivery passion, a shape gliding closer,
skin punctured, horror, the terrible release
as they float up again to the surface.

She borrows an endless array of tools
when his wife is on shift at the hospital,
and slips back through the garage
with hatchets, herbicides, to be returned
next Saturday. I ask her how he got those scars.
escalator. she sighs, *when he was four.* so I know
she's run her tongue over them
and it's already over.

Now she spends Saturdays shopping.
I help her carry a shaky tower of parcels
down the escalator. Her eyes are glassy,
staring at pencil-thin green light between steps
as though she wants to lie down and give up,

lie down with her eye to the slit
and see what lies beneath this suburb,
give herself again, completely this time,
like he did;   our neighbour,
gripped and spit out with scars,
but no memory of what he saw there.

model home 4

All my father wants is to sail down that river
and out of our lives.   He finds a way, finally,
late winter afternoons,
building his boat in the backyard,
standing inside the awful ribs in the last light
with that stoic look on his face,

as though it has swallowed him already
and will deliver him to some other shore.
I thought he was building a dinosaur,
something obsolete, and so did she
when he scavenged useless junk from the cupboards,
but he finds something teeming inside,
swelling its great silk sails.

He uses her wedding dress too,
after she threw it down the stairs in a rage.
Two years later the dress resurfaces,
expensive pure silk cut into patches
for his sail. Evenings,
he sits in the garage with his curved needle,
patiently binding one ripped surface to another,
humming with his work like a coroner, finishing up.

the girl in the reproduction room

The only way I can stay on my feet until five
is to imagine this machine
makes love to me.

It throbs with my touch,
rocking hot against my thighs,
beam of light pulling, pushing me away
trying to make a perfect copy
of itself.

Sometimes I imagine a face.

The light in the bar after work
is the same phosphorescent green
between pulses of dark, and the men
I meet, so smooth
my handprints exude oily heat
smudging their glassy skins.

I only remember the names
of their departments:
customs
and excise, internal affairs.
The timing goes wrong, the skin
pulls up and away too soon
and the light is a slash of blindness
giving nothing back.

A memo descends by elevator
at one minute past five.
I hold my hand over as though checking
a pulse, and slipping from its side
hot as from heaven
are these regulations, these commands.

a handful of keys

Having paused at the illuminated glass
and grappled through purses for our keys,
holding them taut in our hands
before we cross the threshold into darkness.
Alert, sending out soundings,
two women walking to our cars at night.

We would hide this from our friends who are men,
feign a relaxed absentmindedness,
the keys tossed in the air
until we turn the corner and brace ourselves,
keys glinting under streetlights.

She is parked below Parliament Hill,
I am at the dead end of Sparks.
We'll separate at the next corner
and for a few minutes heighten our senses further
still.   Listening for that faint familiar
voice, our mothers calling us at dark,
our sister surfacing from a nightmare.
A cry we will turn towards instinctively.

On our rings, the keys to our usual haunts
and one we cannot identify, slender and
archaic, a skeleton key we might yet
find some use for.
Finding some way to enter him,
to change him with words alone,
reasonable, asking: *why?* while we fiddle
with tarnished metal in the half-light.

But Diana will have none of it.
She raises her keys in her fist.
In his eye,   if she has to.
In the balls,   if that's what he wants,
remind him of what he would have us never forget,
that we are just gristle and matted hair
and sphincters tight with fear.

Each woman we pass carries keys in her hand,
still hoping for the possibility
of sanctuary.   The key to pass soundlessly
out of our world
like the luminous slow flakes falling
around us, touching wet streets,
disappearing without a trace,
and make it to her car.   Its tiny dim halo
of safety.   To that magic threshold of light
she calls home.

I once had a mother

I once had a mother whose hands
smelled of ginger.
All night, rain pattered on the tin roof.
Her spicy smell rose from the earth
as I dozed, and I could see her eyes
when she was far away, like my own,
creased almost shut, as though she was smiling
even when no-one was watching.

I once had a mother with brown hands
who could soothe the distant guns in my head
to a lullaby, whose black hair
was a curtain, dimming
the glow of a burning village on the horizon.

I once had a mother, and then,
I had none,
and each called herself *none*
gliding between the metal beds
never touching any of us, just leaving behind
their scent of dead flowers,
draped in black, beads at their sides clicked
like the teeth of my mother,
her blood seeping onto my mat.
She had a hole in her side,
like Jesus.

I look for her still on the streets
of this city where they brought me
after they promised her soul lives everlastingly,
so I look for her standing in the doorways of bars,
perhaps dressed in black.

I have the penny she gave me,
dark as my hand, with its angry bearded man
gazing over the heads of the people
in some distant country.
This coin, once warmed by her hand,
and this little paper umbrella, once yellow,
from the army bar, that nudged her lips,
now the colour of ash,
and this glass eye from the broken doll
sent by kind Christians, are with me still.

At night I touch these things
that were once my hidden, my only possessions.
By day, the factory brims with toys.
Each shift, a thousand white lambs
glide on their conveyor belt
and I tie white ribbons with bells
around each woolly neck
before they turn their backs on me,
tiny bells tinkling,
like the far-off churches all over America.

Buzzards' Bay

broken rock   heaped
beneath the metal gallows
of a water-tower
Buzzards' Bay in black paint
aimed at the sea

there are no striped gazebos
along shore
so much death rolling   sucked at
nudged forward
to be stepped over

she cannot forget the smell

a fish bloated
round as a man's severed arm

Not feeling so good, honey ?
name from her childhood
though her father turns his grey face
away
swings the car inland
the needle on the dash
points gently at both of them
and gives up its sea pull

to the lopsided tent
metal poles tied with rope
leaning by the tepid lake

near the reeds
smelling like unwashed sheets
she eases her thighs
above the bloodline
where her father's crooked cells swarm

by midnight she is blind
eyes swollen shut
ears ringing with fever
shivering in the locked car

he took his bottle to the next trailer where plastic lanterns bright
and hard as smarties were looped in dense branches of a tower-
ing pine   laughed too loud behind the tiny metal door   a har-
monica chugging over crackling speakers filtered down   the
whine of a trapped insect in the car's vents   then hot lights cut
off   she crawled into the unzipped tent   into the humid sickly
sweet darkness   the private ripping sound of the zipper   cheek
to metal   the dreams she couldn't avoid already drilling invisible
around her head   little stings she slapped away   pushed back
black weight   his white belly shuddered   her eyesight returned
as a rusty sky lowered stinking of mothballs   a turtle outside the
webbed window extended and raised its fleshy head   slow pulse
out of the shell nudged dawn

> still ahead of her
> is the clean white beach
> she imagines
>
> she'll walk far out on the bank
> till she can't see land
> or him   belly down on a towel
> reading *Last Tango in Paris*
>
> the sea will lift her by the neck
> and set her down
> will slap her with waves
> jerk back her head with ammonia spirits

up and down
rhythmic as lovers still ahead
tug
separating head from body
like being born
a series of gentle hangings
her legs will swing in the undertow
feet find rippled sand
before she is hanged again
and each rope will dissolve

her arms around her father's neck as he swam   cheek
against his warm shoulder   speckled from the sun like a
trout   his strokes were strong and safe no matter the depth
before the lines were thrown over his face like a net he
struggled against   and gave up night after night   limp
and bloated in his chair   then the fishing line with its
eel that whipped her legs with horror   the twisted
rope fell away from the tent she left that morning sagging
under the dew

her body tips face down
she parts the waters with her hands
and her feet
for the first time
do not swing

they   kick

IV
Generation

generation

once   your heart was fixed above me   a planet
ringing its clear crystal note   through the firmament
before my syncopated beat   thickened and slowed
leaving this static between us   a humming
in the kitchen   and your broom circles   like radar
searching out invisible specks   you wish
I had never arrived   at this point   so you
could continue   undisturbed

but I want to know   about the chasm   of shivering air
that split us   light shrivelling my wet skin
one late afternoon   in the fall   that Sputnik
was cradled on its way   to the airfield   a searing flame
launched it into the atmosphere   as the gas mask
swept you away   from my first cry   one faint decibel
of a sonic boom   that became a generation

can you hear me   above the hiss   of powerlines   that arc
black   over your neighbourhood   my childhood darkened
by hairline fractures   of outer space   seeping
into daylight   the strange humming of my body
makes you look away   rain that fell on the way to school
still glowing   hot   in my cells   ashes
easy to carbon date a millennium from now   my body
pushed from you   in queer twilight sleep
will return   to the sky one day   a sour smudge of smoke

look up   mother   if only once   before we go
our separate ways   look up   through the air
hazy   with interference   there is this speck
standing before you   a bright flash   almost beautiful
that you must register   passing   across your evening sky

legacy

dragging your feet through snow
so cold   your eyelashes
bead into icy flashes of blindness

you imagine your mother
waiting for your touch on the bell
her soft body
yielding in your small arms

but where is her china face
cool to your fingertips
eyes staring forever ahead
with their irises like shattered glass

where is her chilly head today?

    it is lying under the stars
    filling up with snow
    the wind trapped behind her teeth
    sounds over and over   the same vowel

you wonder again   as you push
against the locked door
where could her head be today?

    it is lying in the root cellar
    at grandmother's farm
    and the pale tubers float up
    searching for soil they will never find

(actually, she is lying intact on her bed
 scribbling as fast as she can:

notes — a woman in danger of the simplest things.

    — she reaches out to touch cut flowers,
            they spit blue sparks at her palm.

    — she knocks over a glass of water,
            and it bursts into flames

    — *don't lose this thought.*

as the bell rings once more.)

you bend to push open the letter slot
with your thick mitten,
calling *Mom   Mom*
like a mournful vengeful wind

closer   your blind mouth reaches
then with just a brush
your lips bond with icy metal
and you tear away without a moment's
thought

now your cry is a wail
and she rushes to you
blots the crimson streaming down
your throat   but it will not clot

you need to tell her how much it hurts
but she presses a cloth over your mouth
shh   she warns you   *don't say anything
or it will never stop*

listening to my mother play

No matter what others say of her,
this is the best she could have offered.
Once, I heard someone in a pew behind me
remark: *She's a cold fish, isn't she?*
and it's so true that even I imagine her
living in a slippery streamlined privacy
not possible in our thin air.

Effortlessly, she sends signals
with her finger slipping over keys
like a startled school of fish
and all that surfaces are orderly rings
long after she's moved along
through her solitary element
in which sound can kill or caress.

What desolation that winter her hands failed,
fingers stiff, stumbling over notes.
Then silence hung over us, a dull icy fog.
Arthritis.   Nothing could melt the ice
in that word, not the flame under paraffin,
dipping her fingers again and again,
ice hardening around the joints.

She wanted nothing but to slip back
into her world
of vague shapes and wordless songs.
By the light of those strange candles,
her hands, idle with wax,
I prayed secretly along with her
that she would again be able to send her love.

Listen.   Her music swirls through the rank air,
eddying us into its current
while all the Christmas candles shimmer.
Their flames swim upwards like bright fish
towards light and nourishment,
a thousand silver scales breaking surface,
rushing upwards, towards the rest of us.

around the water table

earth purifies all things
depth times distance
and poisons
crystallize into stasis
forgetting all their mischief
depth times distance   and pain
melts from limbs
along with flesh and memory
around the water table
we all level out   purified
eventually

this silence between us
how far down does it go
the surface of our skin
is gritty with discontent
morning crumbs under our elbows
as we sit across the table
from one another
you   needing caffeine   before
you start in arguing again
depth times distance
the old measure of how far
we take our differences too

then the change   unbidden
he rises behind your eyes
and draws from me
the slippery message
from the water table
and she rises to you
an eerie current running deep
making you shiver
long after we are dissolved
these two will find
their way to each other
through any bedrock

shadow

Your absence stretches ahead of me
like this late afternoon shadow.

I tear green veins from soil as it falls
leaching red from petals, but never

have I been more aware of your body:
chest hairs cutting my cheek

I listen to your heart, a shudder
passing under the earth. Still

I can turn my back and squint
into the jubilant light, risk

stumbling over dailiness, but always
a dark stain seeps from my gashed heel.

How we began: negatives falling from shelves
scatter among next fall's stored bulbs

and there are my red lips drained, ghastly
train of my dress, a shadow, and you

my husband, beside me in your good suit
bleaching into nothingness.

insemination

this calf has shattered
the frozen heavens
constellations
swing away from their fixed codes
spill down a glass tunnel
and he drops on New Year's Day
into an icy puddle
in the cratered barnyard
with the sound of splintering
glass

his father has been dead
for twenty years
the last bull your father
shoved affectionately
in and out the barn door
two old patriarchs
jostling through their last fall
together on earth

you and your brother
scratch his wiry belly
congratulate each other
and slap his flank
sure that this season of calves
will be the best yet
strong neck muscles
sturdy front legs you recognize
from your adolescence
your father's mighty bull
resurrected

only memory is possible now
your father cannot return
locked behind the mirror
you face each morning
so you lean closer
to hear him laugh along
at this victory
this calf hurtled into life
through his mother
who stoops to lick blood
from his dazed eyes

la petite mort

uncurling papery shrouds
the moths emerge   creeping slowly
along folds of sheets

their wings drag
leaving silver threads of dust
along our skins

so faint
they may be only tricks
the mind plays

but I move you over me
a drowsy hand sweeping your spine
a moth flies up

your unshaven cheek
brushes my neck   a moth
flies up

your hands catch in my hair
the moths fly up
then flutter   phosphorescent

before dissolving
into the blackness
above our bed

when you lift   finally
slipping out of me   and tremble
pale   on your knees

this is my little death
not our shuddering communion
but this slackening

my body   relinquished   as you rise
lightened   and move towards
the dark heaven of sleep

poetry

the opening of veins
is only half of it
who receives   receives

without a face
receives and rises
renewed

believe that dark words
spill onto a tragedy
and turn it around

believe that it moves
by some divine force
into the air

and onwards
into others' veins   just
when they need it most

when they've never been
so frightened
when their child's heart beats

in someone's gloved hands
there are no words in this
transfusion

just pure generosity
passing from one unconscious
body to another

lifting us from our fainting
so that we press hands
to our temples   saying:

I don't know
what came over me,
but I'm all right now.